To Justin Chanda, editor extraordinaire,
who always makes me feel like I'm floating
(in a good way)
—A. R.

For Ginny Ridpath, with much love
—D. R. O.

ACKNOWLEDGMENTS

The illustrator thanks Laurent Linn, Justin Chanda,
and Alexa Pastor at Simon & Schuster Children's for
helping Bob and his friend Sea Monkey find their way.

SIMON & SCHUSTER BOOKS FOR YOUNG READERS
• An imprint of Simon & Schuster Children's Publishing
Division • 1230 Avenue of the Americas, New York, New
York 10020 • Text copyright © 2017 by Aaron Reynolds •
Illustrations copyright © 2017 by Debbie Ridpath Ohi • All
rights reserved, including the right of reproduction in whole or
in part in any form. • SIMON & SCHUSTER BOOKS FOR YOUNG
READERS is a trademark of Simon & Schuster, Inc. • For information
about special discounts for bulk purchases, please contact Simon &
Schuster Special Sales at 1-866-506-1949 or business@simonandschuster
.com. • The Simon & Schuster Speakers Bureau can bring authors to your live
event. For more information or to book an event, contact the Simon & Schuster
Speakers Bureau at 1-866-248-3049 or visit our website at www.simonspeakers
.com. • Book design by Laurent Linn • The text for this book was set in Ed Gothic and
Joppa. • The illustrations for this book were rendered digitally. • Manufactured in China
• 0217 SCP • 10 9 8 7 6 5 4 3 2 1 • CIP data for this book is available from the
Library of Congress. • ISBN 978-1-4814-0676-5 • ISBN 978-1-4814-0677-2 (eBook)

Sea Monkey & Bob

Aaron Reynolds

Illustrated by Debbie Ridpath Ohi

SIMON & SCHUSTER BOOKS FOR YOUNG READERS

NEW YORK   LONDON   TORONTO   SYDNEY   NEW DELHI

Hi. I am Bob.

I am a puffer fish.

And I am
Sea Monkey.

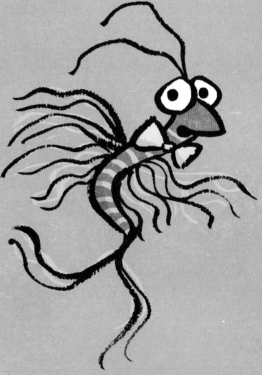

What is wrong, Sea Monkey?

 I aM scaRed.

What is the matter?

I am scared I am going to SINK.

Right down to the bottom of the ocean.

It is DARK at the bottom of the ocean.

I am also scared of the dark.

You will not sink.

I could sink, Bob.
I am Much heavier than I Look.
Heavy things sink.

They do?

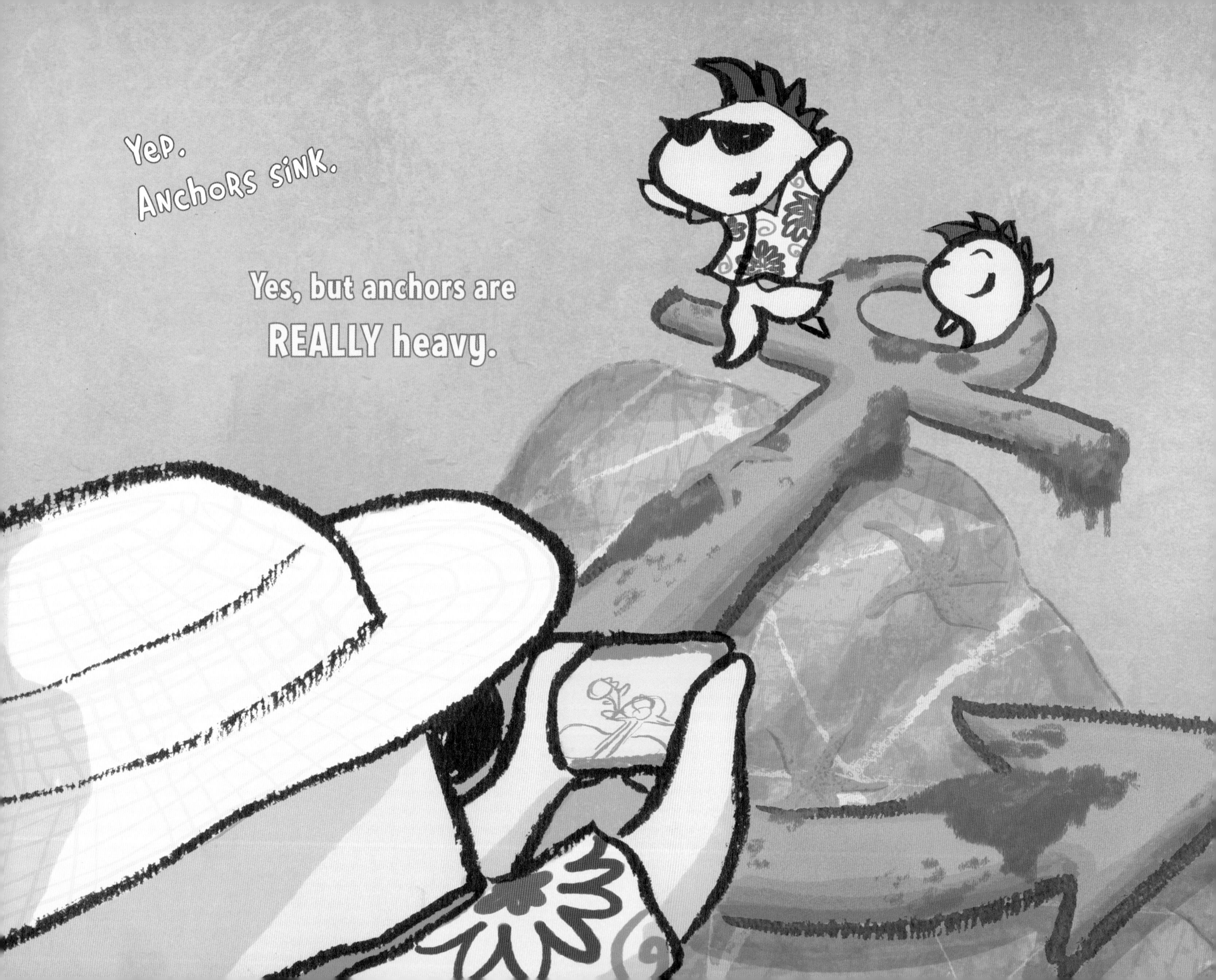
Yep.
Anchors sink.
Yes, but anchors are
REALLY heavy.

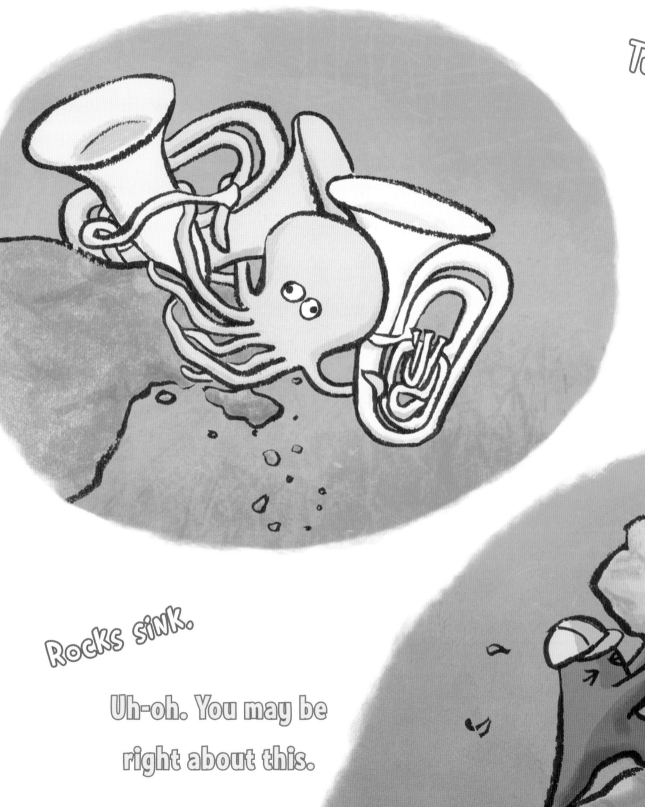

Tubas sink.

Tubas? Really?

I did not know that.

Rocks sink.

Uh-oh. You may be right about this.

DINOSAURS SINK.

You have never
seen a dinosaur.

Now *I* am nervous.

Why?

YOU aRe Not heavy.

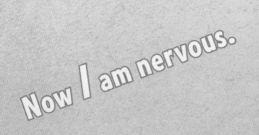

I am scared I am going to **float**.

?

Float?

I am a very light fish.

I could float right up to the surface.

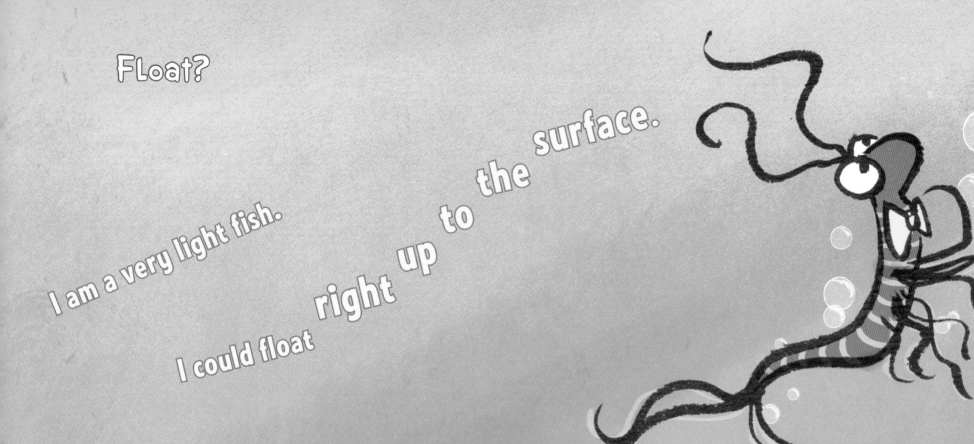

There is air at the surface.

I am scared of the air.

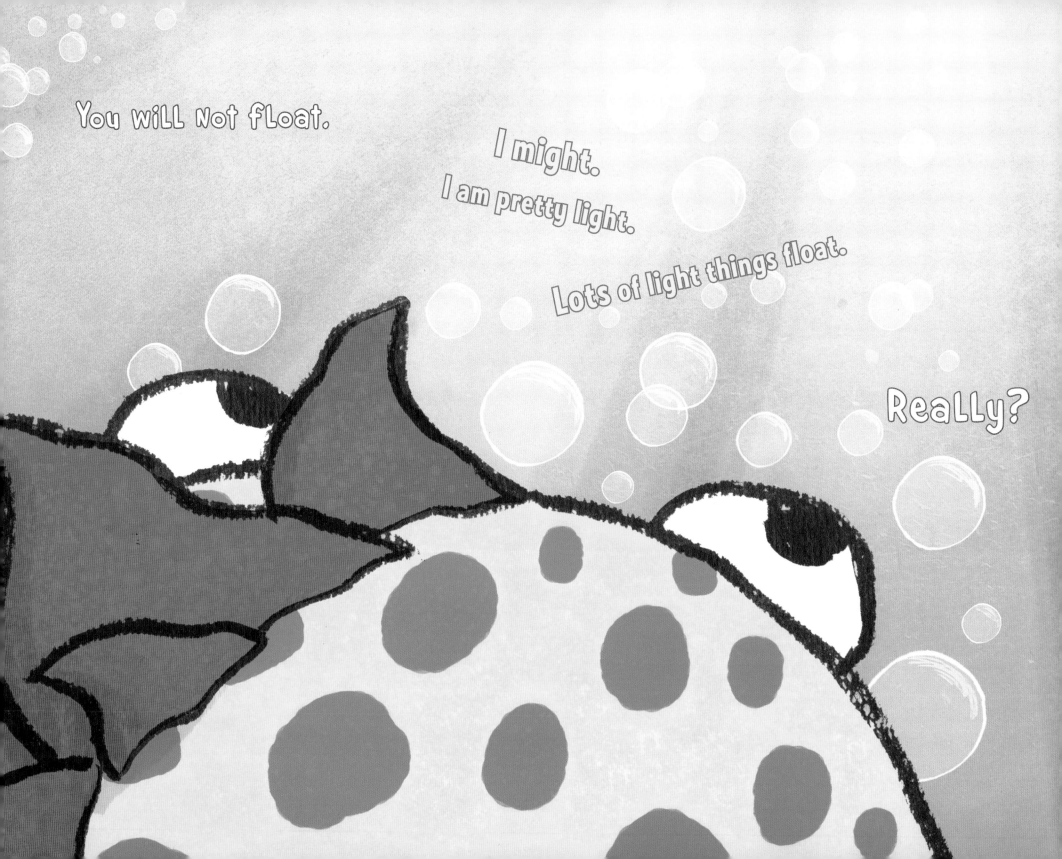

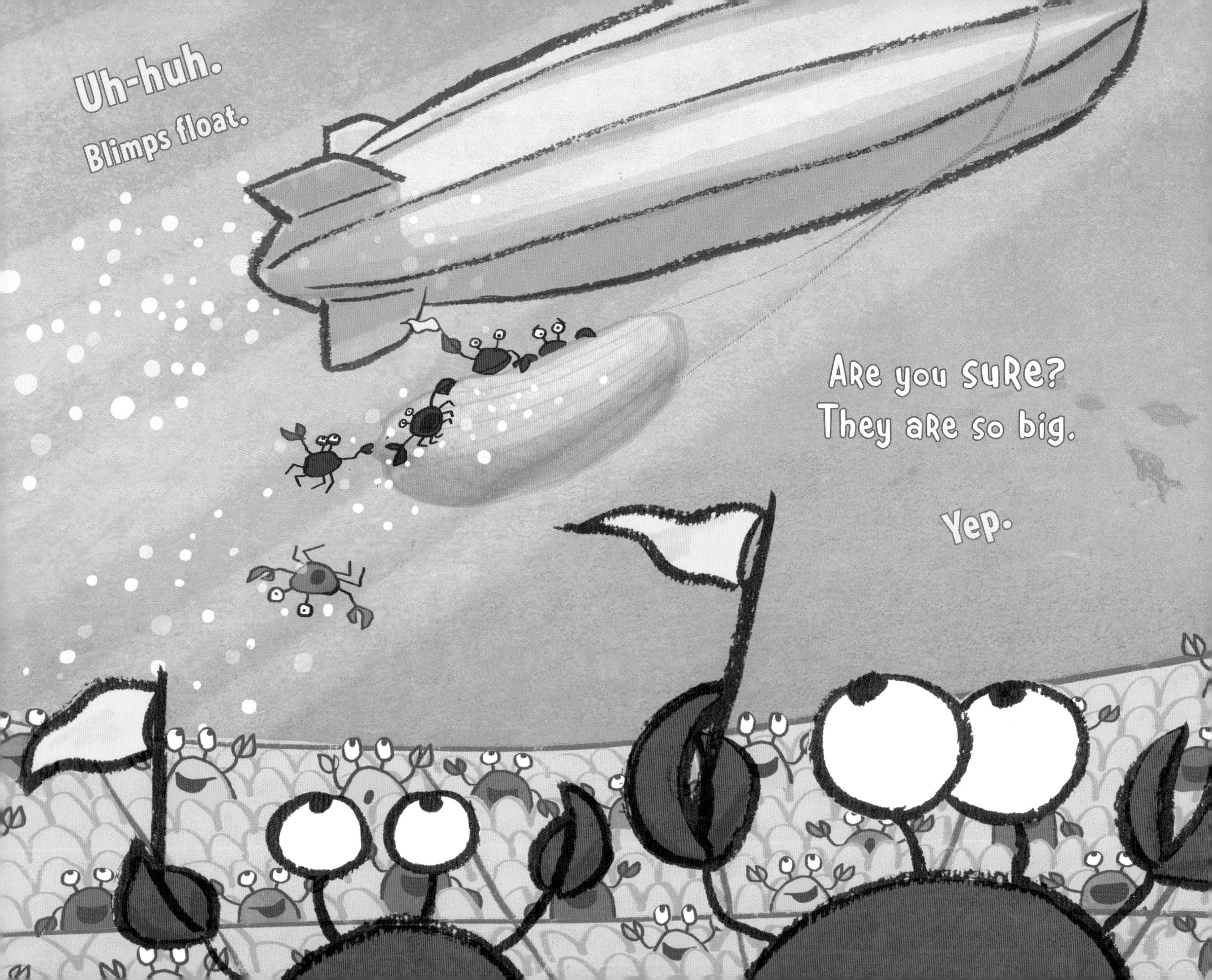

Uh-huh.
Blimps float.

Are you SURE?
They are so big.

Yep.

Pumpkins float.

Pumpkins are
Not Light.

They still float.

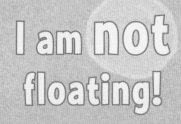

I am **not** floating!

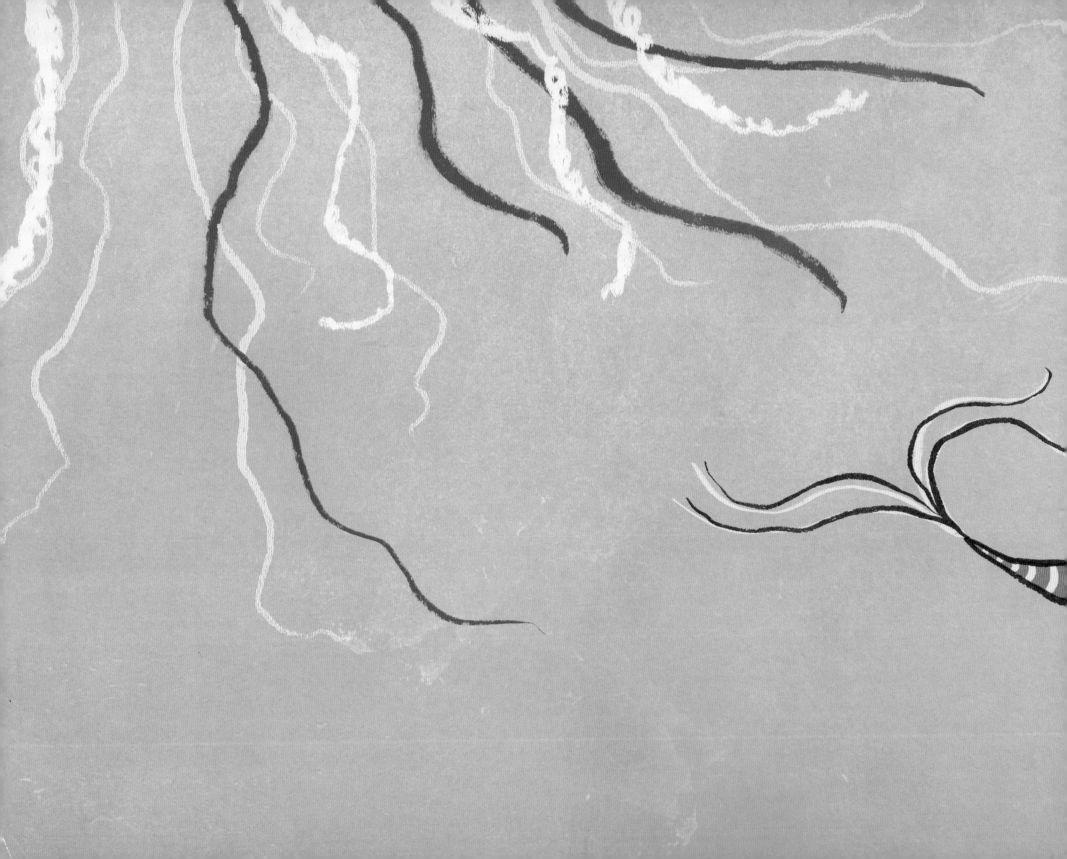

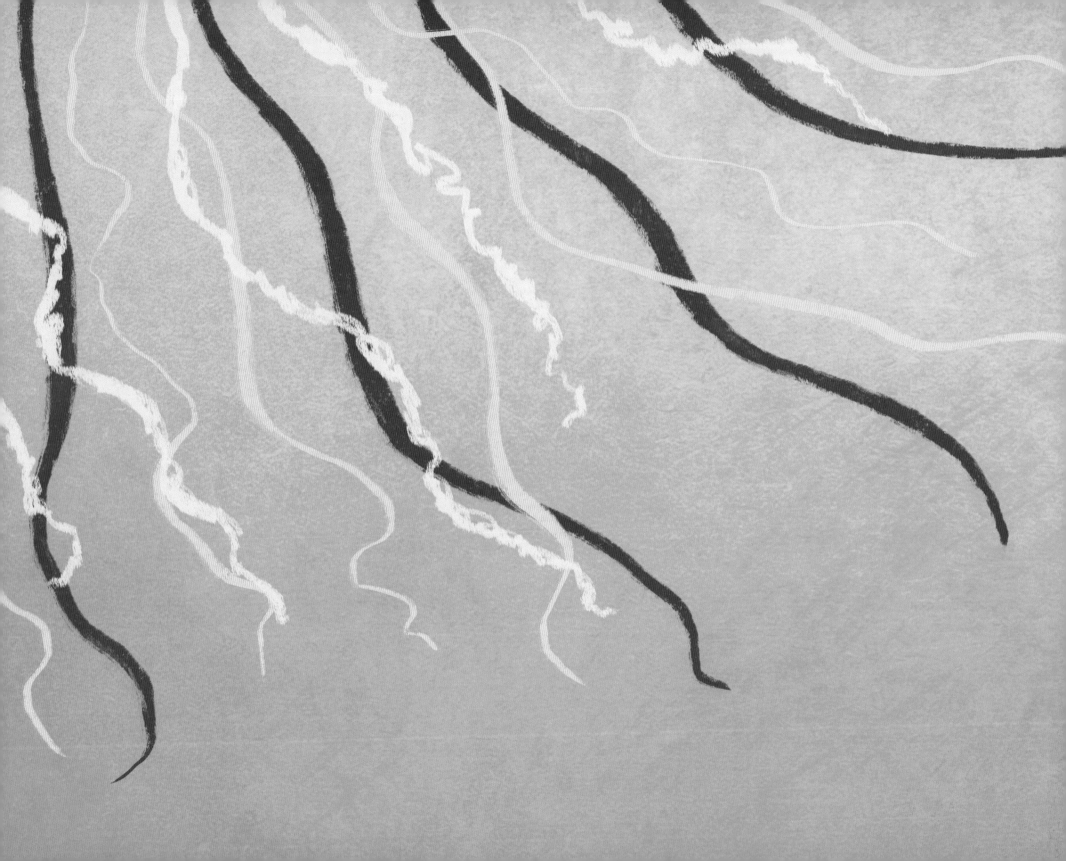

Except for jellyfish.

I am STILL SCARED
of jellyfish.

I think it is the stingers.

And they are gooey.

Yep.
Jellyfish are SCARY.

Do **not** be scared of jellyfish,

Sea Monkey.

Why not?

Jellyfish float.

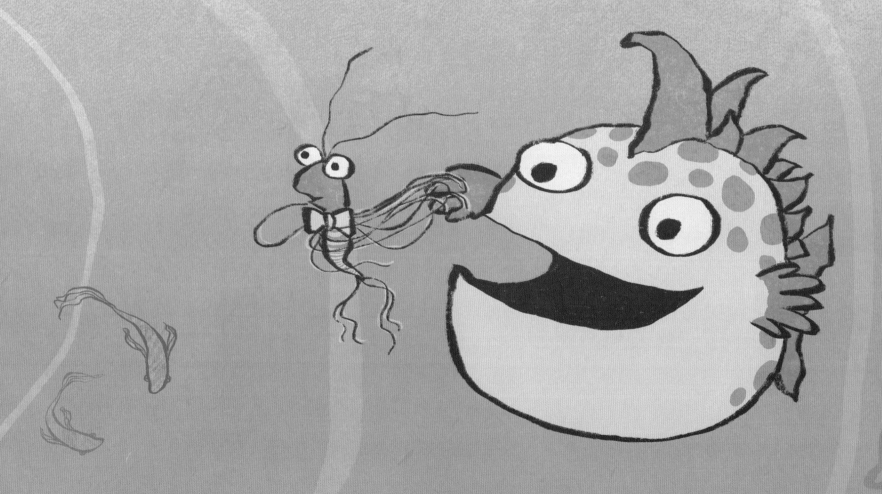

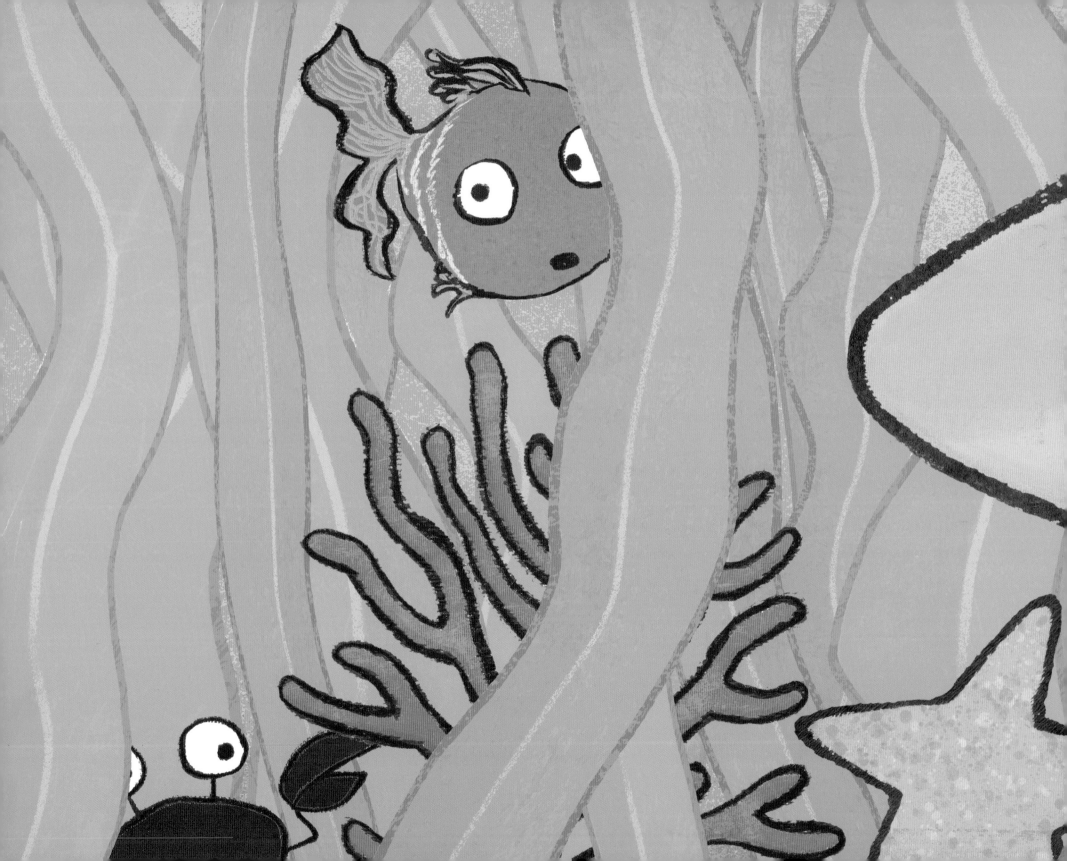